## ABOUT THE BANK STREET READY-TO-READ SERIES

More than seventy-five years of educational research, innovative teaching, and quality publishing have earned The Bank Street College of Education its reputation as America's most trusted name in early childhood education.

Because no two children are exactly alike in their development, the Bank Street Ready-to-Read series is written on three levels to accommodate the individual stages of reading readiness of children ages three through eight.

○ *Level 1:* GETTING READY TO READ (Pre-K–Grade 1)
Level 1 books are perfect for reading aloud with children who are getting ready to read or just starting to read words or phrases. These books feature large type, repetition, and simple sentences.

● *Level 2:* READING TOGETHER (Grades 1–3)
These books have slightly smaller type and longer sentences. They are ideal for children beginning to read by themselves who may need help.

○ *Level 3:* I CAN READ IT MYSELF (Grades 2–3)
These stories are just right for children who can read independently. They offer more complex and challenging stories and sentences.

All three levels of The Bank Street Ready-to-Read books make it easy to select the books most appropriate for your child's development and enable him or her to grow with the series step by step. The levels purposely overlap to reinforce skills and further encourage reading.

We feel that making reading fun is the single most important thing anyone can do to help children become good readers. We hope you will become part of Bank Street's long tradition of learning through sharing.

The Bank Street College of Education

*For young Robert — S. R.*

*For Tommy — K. F.*

For a free color catalog describing Gareth Stevens' list of high-quality books and
multimedia programs, call 1-800-542-2595 (USA) or 1-800-461-9120 (Canada).
Gareth Stevens Publishing's Fax: (414) 225-0377.
See our catalog, too, on the World Wide Web: http://gsinc.com

Library of Congress Cataloging-in-Publication Data

Reit, Seymour.
    A dog's tale / by Seymour Reit ; illustrated by Kate Flanagan.
      p.  cm. -- (Bank Street ready-to-read)
      Summary: A puppy is adopted by a little girl who is not experienced with pets, so the
dog must teach her everything she needs to know to take care of him properly.
      ISBN 0-8368-1615-3 (lib. bdg.)
      [1. Dogs--Fiction.  2. Animals--Infancy--Fiction.  3. Pets--Fiction.]  I. Flanagan, Kate, ill.
II. Title.  III. Series.
PZ7.R2785Do  1996
[E]--dc20                                    96-6877

This edition first published in 1996 by
**Gareth Stevens Publishing**
1555 North RiverCenter Drive, Suite 201
Milwaukee, Wisconsin 53212 USA

Printed in Mexico

2 3 4 5 6 7 8 9 99 99 98

Bank Street Ready-to-Read™

# A DOG'S TALE

by Seymour Reit
Illustrated by Kate Flanagan

A# 00-217

A Byron Preiss Book

Gareth Stevens Publishing
MILWAUKEE

When I was a tiny puppy,
I lived at the pound.
But I was very lonely.
I wanted a person to love—
a person all my own.

Then, one wonderful day,
I saw Wendy.
She was just right for me!
So I let her take me home.

Wendy was a good kid,
but she never had a puppy before.
She had lots to learn.
Lucky she had me to teach her!

First I helped her pick my name.
She called me Spot, then Skippy.
When she called me Ruff
I barked, "Ruff! Ruff! Ruff!"

I had to teach her that puppies
eat at least three times a day.
I always remind her
if she forgets!

8

I even had to teach Wendy
that puppies need
lots of fresh water.

Wendy finally got the hang of it.
She found a big box and
made a warm, cozy bed for me.

But sometimes I just have to
snuggle in Wendy's bed.
It makes her so happy!

Chewing is good
for a puppy's teeth.
I pointed out
my favorites to Wendy.

She wagged her finger at me
and showed me *her* favorites:
old socks, rubber balls,
and toy bones.

I like to take Wendy for walks,
but I always put her on a leash.
This keeps her from getting lost
or running out into traffic.

Sometimes we meet my friend Rags
and his nice person, Carlo.
Carlo always trips over his leash.
Rags will just have to train him!

Wendy and I love to go to the park
where we can run and play.

Lots of dogs come
to show off their people.

We let our owners off their leashes
while Wendy gets pet tips.

Then we dogs run around
and have sniffing contests.

I'm teaching Wendy lots of
good games—like fetch.
First I make her throw a stick.

Then I run and pick it up
so she can throw it again.

She's getting very good at it!

I often bark and wag my tail
to show Wendy when I'm happy.
It's good to praise your person!

I also show Wendy when I'm mad.
I chew one of her good shoes,
or I leave a puddle on the floor.

I'm teaching Wendy puppy talk, too.
When I bring the leash, it means
I want to take her outside.

When I roll over on my back,
I want my belly scratched.

24

I'm learning people talk, too.
I know "sit" and "good dog."
But my favorite word is "walk."

I'm trying to teach Wendy
how much I hate baths.
I splash a lot to make sure
she gets good and wet, too.

26

I leave lots of paw prints
all over the towels and floor.
I give myself a big shake.
It makes such a nice wet mess!

One day Wendy brought home
a tiny black kitten.
I tried to teach Wendy
a lesson she wouldn't forget:
I DON'T LIKE CATS!

I barked at it.
I growled at it.
But it just curled up in a ball
and purred.

For days it rubbed up against me
and licked my face.
Did this kitten like me?
Could we get along?

30

I decided that two tails
are better than one.
And here's the happy ending
of this dog's tale:

We put our paws together
and taught Wendy
how to take care of *both* of us.
Ruff! Meow!